Roger Hurn used to be an actor in 'The Exploding Trouser Company'. He has also appeared on 'The Weakest Link' on TV – and he won!

Now he spends his time writing and telling stories. His scariest and spookiest experience came when he went to an old ghost town in the Wild West of the USA. This gave him the idea for **Spook Squad**.

He hopes you enjoy reading the Spook Squad's adventures as much as he enjoyed writing them.

Spook Squad
Ghouls in School
by Roger Hurn
Illustrated by Peter Richardson

Published by Ransom Publishing Ltd.
Radley House, 8 St. Cross Road, Winchester, Hampshire
SO23 9HX, UK
www.ransom.co.uk

ISBN   978 184167 072 0
First published in 2012

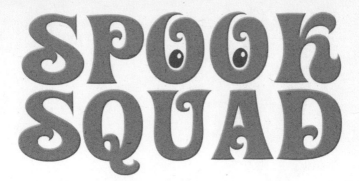

Ghouls

in

School

by Roger Hurn

Ransom

DEAD END
JUNCTION

Vlad the
Bad's
Castle

THE GHOST
TRAIN RAILWAY

GHOULS'
GRAVEYARD

THE ISLE OF
FRIGHT

It's the dead
centre of
Otherworld!

THE WRAITH PITS
They really
are the pits!

THE HAUNTED PYRAMID

Your mummy warned
you about this place

HERE THERE
BE DRAGONS

BANSHEE BAY
Where the wind
never stops howling!

They sleep in the day
and fight knights!

Otherworld

GOBLIN GULCH
The home of
messy eaters

FANG MOUNTAINS
You'll say 'Fangs for
nothing' if you try to
climb them

KRAKEN LAKE

Swim at
your
own risk!

SPOOK CITY

THE ZOMBI RIVER

WEREWOLF WOODS
Avoid when the
moon is full!

Otherworld

Where is Otherworld?

> The far side of a shadow.

Who lives there?

> Ghouls, ghosts, long-leggedy beasties and things that go bump in the night.

Why do the creatures who live there come to our world?

> To make mischief.

Rhee the Banshee answers readers' questions.

How do they get here?

> They slip through secret gateways when you're not looking.

Can humans go to Otherworld?

> Yes, but they shouldn't.

Why not?

> Because they never come back.

Why not?

> Trust me – you really **DO NOT** want to know!

Meet The SPOOK SQUAD

Emma

FYI: She spends her life getting hold of the wrong end of the stick.

Loves: Getting the point.

Hates: Muddy sticks.

Fact: She doesn't like vampires – she thinks they're a pain in the neck.

Roxy

FYI: Don't call her 'Ginger' – unless you want to eat your dinner through a straw.

Loves: Being a strawberry blonde.

Hates: Seeing red.

Fact: She reckons cannibal goblins are messy eaters, so she won't be joining their fang club.

Nita

FYI: This girl gets gadgets. Give her a paper clip, a rubber band, a tin can and an A4 battery and she'll rig up a gizmo that'll blow your gran's pop socks off.

Loves: Fixing things.

Hates: Fixing it – if it ain't broke.

Fact: Nita has invented ghost-proof wheels for her bike. They don't have any spooks!

Leena

FYI: If she was any sharper you could use her to slice bread.

Loves: Big words.

Hates: Small minds.

Fact: She prefers whatwolves and whenwolves to werewolves.

Aunt Rhee

FYI: Rhee's not the kind of aunt who gives you a woolly jumper for Christmas.

Loves: Walking on the wild side.

Hates: Things that go bump in the night.

Fact: Rhee is just too cool for ghouls.

Rattle

FYI: Rattle says he's a poltergeist. He thinks poltergeists are posher than ghosts.

Loves: Boo-berry pie and I-scream.

Hates: People who sneak up behind him and shout BOO!

Fact: Rattle's only happy when he's moaning.

Interview with a Poltergeist

Rattle answers readers' questions.

Have you always haunted the Old Tower?

No, I used to haunt the graveyard.

So why did you move?

Are you kidding? I was dying to get away. That graveyard was way too creepy for me.

Are you a scary ghost?

No, I won't say boo to a goose ... unless it really deserves it.

What do you think of the Spook Squad?

They're too cheeky. They shouldn't spook until they are spooken to.

Does Aunt Rhee mind a ghost like you haunting her house?

No, but I'm not allowed in the living room.

Do you think the spooks will ever beat the Spook Squad?

No, they haven't got a ghost of a chance.

The Ghoul

Description: Very creepy.

Strength: It can chill your blood.

Weakness: It's a dead loss.

Likes:
Demons – because demons are a ghoul's best friend.

Hates: School dinners.

What to do if you see a ghoul:
Tell it you're not looking for a ghoul friend.

Scream Scale Rating:
It's too ghoul for school!

Chapter One

The Practical Jokers

It was lunchtime at the Spook Squad's school. Roxy, Emma, Leena and Nita were in for a surprise.

'I don't believe it!' Leena stared at her locker in disgust. 'Someone has put superglue in my locker keyhole!'

'No way! Why would anyone do that?' said Roxy.

'I don't know, do I?' snapped Leena. 'But

it means I can't open my locker and my lunch is in there!'

This was a major problem. Leena loved her grub. She once even tried to eat her homework when Miss Raven said it was a piece of cake.

'Don't worry, Lee, you can share my lunch.' Emma smiled sweetly at her friend. 'It's ever so healthy. I've got lettuce sandwiches and a nut bar with lots of seeds.'

Leena glared at her. 'Hey, do I have brightly coloured feathers, a sharp beak and say *'Who's a pretty boy then?'* every two minutes?'

Emma looked puzzled. 'Er … no.'

'Then don't offer me parrot food!' snarled Leena. 'I'm starving and I want

pizza and chocolate fudge cake.'

Nita clicked her fingers. 'No problem,
Lee. I know how we can unglue the lock.'

'Brilliant,' said Leena. 'How?'

'All we need is cooking oil and lots of patience.'

'But we don't have any cooking oil,' said Roxy.

'And Leena certainly hasn't got any patience,' said Emma.

'Well, let's hope the rest of you have,' said Leena. 'Because the joker who stuck up my locker has done the same to all yours!'

The girls groaned. Then Emma spotted a small, yellow tube on the floor.

'Look at this,' she said. 'Whoever stuck up the lockers is also a litter lout. They've left the superglue behind.'

Just then Mr Bull, their headteacher, came hurrying down the corridor.

'What's going on here?' he growled.

Chapter Two

A Sticky Situation

'Why are you girls hanging around the lockers? You should be in the dining hall eating your packed lunches by now.'

'We would be, sir,' said Emma, 'but someone's glued our lockers shut. Look!'

Mr Bull peered at the keyholes. Then he spotted the tube of superglue in Emma's hand.

'Ah ha!' he exclaimed. 'So you girls are

the practical jokers I'm after.'

'What are you on about, sir?' asked Roxy. 'Someone's glued up our lockers – but it wasn't us.'

'Really?' said Mr Bull. 'And I suppose it wasn't you who mixed up the chemicals Mr Dreyfus used in his science lesson this morning.'

'No – but what happened?' asked Nita.

'The chemicals exploded and blew Mr Dreyfus' wig off. Now he's as bald as a billiard ball!' bellowed Mr Bull.

The girls gasped in horror.

'We didn't do it,' said Roxy. 'But, Mr Bull, even if we were the practical jokers, why would we glue our own lockers?'

'To throw me off the scent,' he barked. 'But luckily I came along at just the right moment to catch you red-handed. Now, go to my office at once!'

• • • • •

When they all arrived at Mr Bull's office, he wrenched the door open. A bucket filled with icy water came crashing down on his head.

'ARRRRGH!' he screamed.

The practical jokers had struck again!

'Oh fiddlesticks!' screeched a ghostly voice. The girls looked up and saw Rattle hovering just below the ceiling. He made an '*It wasn't me*' face at them and flew off down the corridor. Then the Spook Squad heard shrieks of terror coming from the

hall. Mr Bull pulled the bucket off his head.

'What on Earth is going on?' he spluttered.

'I don't know,' said Roxy, 'but we're going to find out. Come on guys!'

Chapter Three

Disaster in the Dining Hall

'I knew Rattle had to be the practical joker,' said Roxy, as the Spook Squad ran down the corridor towards the hall.

'So did I,' said Leena. 'He loves playing stupid pranks.'

'Yes, he's always sneaking up on me and shouting *'Boo!'*" sniffed Emma.

'Well,' said Nita. 'That poltergeist has just made one boo boo too many.'

'Too right,' said Leena. 'That ghost is toast when I get my hands on him!'

The Spook Squad burst into the dining hall, but suddenly their feet shot out from under them. They went crashing down and slithered along on their bottoms.

'YUK!' squealed Emma. The floor was awash with mashed potato and turkey twizzlers floating on a sea of banana custard.

'Quick! Hide under here before the monsters get you!' hissed a scared voice.

The Spook Squad saw that all the children were under the dining tables, along with the dinner ladies.

'What the heck is going on?' asked Leena.

'Look!' A horrified dinner lady pointed at the stage at the front of the hall. A bright light was shining behind the closed curtains, and two huge shadows were moving across them.

'Yikes!' said Emma. 'Those monsters lurking behind the curtains must be at least ten feet tall.'

'Maybe,' said Nita. 'But just how is Rattle doing that?'

Suddenly Rattle appeared out of thin air right next to them. The dinner lady fainted.

'I'm not,' he said. 'But I know who is – and you've got to stop them.'

'Stop who?' demanded Leena.

'Sorry to break the bad news, girls,' said the little poltergeist, 'but you've got two ghouls in school. They're the ones who have been playing all the practical jokes. I've been trying to stop them.'

'Well, you haven't done a very good job so far,' said Leena.

'Duh! They're ten feet tall and I'm only little,' said Rattle. 'Anyway, you're the Spook Squad. It's your job to stop ghouls – not mine.'

'We will,' said Leena.

'But how?' said Emma.

'With these,' said Nita. She picked up a plate full of rice pudding and jam. 'It's a well-known fact that ghouls can't stand school rice pudding.'

'Is that true, Nita?' asked Emma.

'Dunno,' replied Nita, 'but *we* all hate it, so it's got to be worth a try.'

'And if it doesn't work, we can always try Plan B,' said Leena.

'What's Plan B?' asked Emma.

'There is no Plan B,' replied Leena. 'So let's just hope Plan A works.'

Chapter Four

Just Desserts

Clutching their plates full of sloppy pudding, the Spook Squad slipped and slithered across the hall.

'Up and at 'em, Spook Squad!' yelled Roxy.

The girls clambered up on to the stage and pushed through the curtains. But they did a double take when they saw two small ghouls prancing about in front of a projector.

It was the projector that made the ghouls' shadows seem so big!

The Spook Squad let fly with their plates of rice pudding.

SPLAT!   SPLAT!

SPLAT!   SPLAT!

They scored four direct hits.

'YUKKKKK!!!!' screeched the ghouls. 'This stuff tastes horrible. BLEUGH!'

'Hey, it works!' yelled Nita.

The two ghouls fled. But they crashed straight into Mr Bull as he stepped up onto the stage.

WHOOOMPH! Mr Bull fell over backwards and the two horrors used his tummy as a trampoline as they leapt down to try and escape.

'STOP THOSE BOYS!' shouted Mr Bull. He struggled back up to his feet and gave chase.

'You got it,' yelled Leena. She scooped up a dish of custard and hurled it as hard as she could.

SPLOSH! It hit Mr Bull and knocked him down again. He fell face-first into a plate of mashed potato and beans.

'Whoops … sorry, sir!' Leena tried hard not to giggle.

The ghouls dashed out of the hall, across the playground and vanished into the park at the end of the street.

The Spook Squad ran up to Mr Bull and helped him up. Mashed potato, beans and custard dribbled down his face.

'Gerroff me,' snarled Mr Bull. 'Who were they?'

'They are the practical jokers,' said Roxy.

'We think they're boys from another school,' said Emma.

'And they were wearing masks as a disguise,' said Nita.

'So I guess we'll never find out who they

39

are,' said Leena.

'Oh yes we will,' snapped Mr Bull. 'I'll phone the other head teachers and tell them to inspect all their boys to see if any of them have rice pudding and custard on their clothes.'

'That's a brilliant idea, sir,' said Emma.

'It is,' agreed Roxy.

'And the other head teachers won't think it's even the tiniest bit weird,' said Nita.

Mr Bull nodded and a lump of mashed potato slid slowly down his forehead. 'No one makes a fool of me and gets away with it,' he said.

'No sir,' said Leena sweetly. 'They certainly don't.'

Chapter Five

Food for Thought

That night the Spook Squad told Auntie Rhee all about their adventure with the two ghoulish practical jokers.

'You were lucky they were only baby ghouls,' said Rhee sternly. 'Ghouls start off playing silly practical jokes, but they soon move on to really dangerous tricks.'

There was a whooshing sound and Rattle appeared in the room.

'Oh don't get your knickers in a twist, Rhee,' he said. 'I had the situation under control the whole time.'

'Oh no you didn't,' said Roxy.

'You were useless,' said Leena.

'And you made one of the dinner ladies faint when you suddenly appeared out of thin air right next to her,' said Emma.

Rhee glared up at Rattle. 'Did you?'

The poltergeist shrugged sulkily. 'No, she was tired and decided to have a very sudden nap.'

Rhee sighed. 'Ghosts should never tell lies, Rattle, because people can see right through them.'

'Don't worry, Rhee. The dinner lady was

all right,' said Nita. 'I told her she hadn't seen a ghost, but just a dirty old dish cloth one of the practical jokers had thrown at her.'

Rattle was furious. 'I look nothing like a dish cloth,' he protested. 'I'm far more handsome.'

'That's right, Rattle' agreed Emma. 'I'd say you were more like a good-looking tea towel.'

Rattle glowered at Emma and then disappeared in a huff.

'Oh no,' she said. 'I've upset him.'

At that very moment an eerie howling echoed through the house.

'Oh don't worry, Em, he's just gone off to have a moan,' said Leena.

Rhee smiled at the girls. 'I'm proud of you girls,' she said. 'Those ghouls won't be back in a hurry.'

'I guess they didn't like the taste of school rice pudding and banana custard,' said Emma.

The banshee grinned. 'And talking of food, why don't we all go into town for a pizza – my treat?'

The girls whooped and high-fived each other.

'Hey,' said Leena, 'I guess it's true: when you outwit ghouls every shroud really does have a silver lining!'

The next Spook Squad adventure is

Bats in the Attic

It's a Scream!

Spook Squad's Scary Joke Page

What happens if you meet twin witches?

You won't be able to tell which witch is which!

What does the postman deliver to vampires?

Fang mail!

What is a ghost's favourite day of the week?

Frightday!